This book belongs to:

_____

_____

The West Forest

Nettie's old house

The Fairy Forest

The Spare Wing shop

Bluebell's toadstool

To the East Forest →

Nettie's New Shoes

Lynda Britnell . Joanna Walsh

Orion
Children's Books

First published in Great Britain in 1996
by Orion Children's Books
a division of the Orion Publishing Group Ltd
Orion House
5 Upper St Martin's Lane
London WC2H 9EA

A catalogue record for this book is available from the British Library
Printed in Great Britain

Nettie Mugwort was a fairy.

But Nettie wasn't an ordinary fairy.
She was taller than an ordinary fairy.
Her hair was spikier
than an ordinary fairy's hair,
in fact rather like a hedgehog.
She had strap-on wings.
And Nettie's feet were bigger
than an ordinary fairy's feet.

In fact... Nettie's feet were three times bigger than an ordinary fairy's feet.

And this was a problem
because none of the shoe shops

had shoes in Nettie's size.
All the shoes she tried on were too small.

So Nettie thought, "I will make my own shoes."
She went into the fairy forest
with a big bag
and collected lots of things.

First Nettie made some shoes
from dandelion seeds.
They looked soft and warm.
But when Nettie put the shoes on,
sand got into them
and tickled her toes.

Next she made some shoes
from sweet chestnut shells.
They wouldn't let the sand in
to tickle her toes.
But when Nettie put them on
she prickled her fingers.
"Ouch!" she said.
"If I trod on someone
I would hurt them."

Last of all
Nettie made some shoes from moss.
They wouldn't hurt
if she trod on someone.
But when she walked out in the rain
the moss got soggy…

and Nettie's feet got wet.

Nettie sat down.
"Oh, what shall I do?"
she said.
Just then she heard a
thump! thump! thump!
It was coming closer:
thump! thump! thump!
And closer: THUMP!
THUMP! THUMP!
And closer: THUMP!
THUMP! THUMP!

Out of the trees came
Know-It-All the Gnome.
He stopped beside Nettie.
"What's wrong?" he said.
Nettie told him all about
her problem feet
and that she couldn't find
any shoes to fit her.

"Your feet aren't a problem,"
said Know-It-All. "Look!
Your feet are the same size as mine."
And when Nettie looked
she saw that they were.
"You just haven't looked in the right place,"
said Know-It-All.
"Come with me."
And that's just what she did.

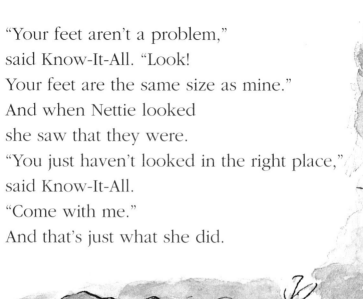

Know-It-All took her to a shop called
Gnome Your Feet.

Gnome Your Feet was a wonderful place.

There were all kinds of shoes.

Big shoes and little shoes,

plain shoes and sparkly shoes.

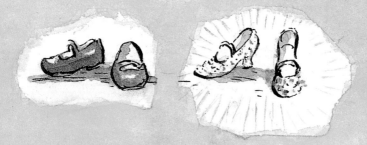

Nettie found a pair of pink
hiking boots that fitted perfectly.

"They may not be as small
as other fairies' shoes," said Nettie.
"But they fit," said Know-It-All.
"And I like them," said Nettie.